Teddy's Favorite Toy

Teddy's Favorite Toy

by Christian Trimmer

illustrated by Madeline Valentine

Atheneum Books for Young Readers
New York London Toronto Sydney New Delhi

Teddy has a lot of cool toys.

Like this one.

And this one

and this one

and this one

and this one

and this one

and this one

and this one.

But this one is his absolute favorite.

Bren-Da, Warrior Queen of Pacifica,
has the best manners.

She has the sickest
fighting skills.

Flying crane spinning split kick!

And she is able to pull off a number
of different looks, like this one.

Yas, queen!

And this one

and this one

and this one

and this one.

One morning, in the middle of a particularly epic battle, this happened.

SNAP!

Teddy tried to fix her,

but to no avail.

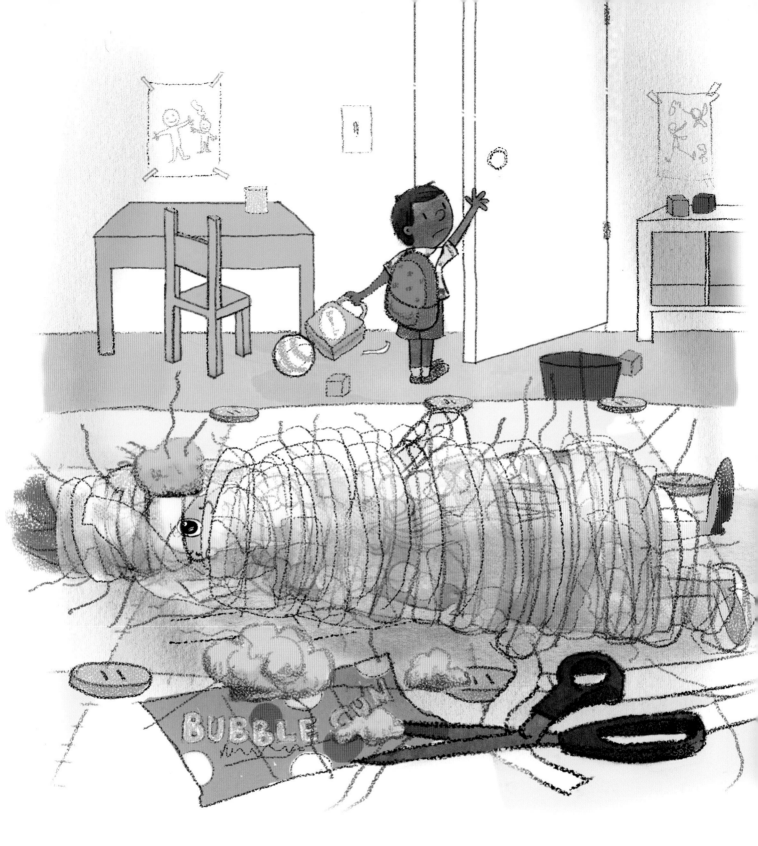

He carefully bandaged her wounds,
vowing to try again later.

Then Teddy headed off
to school . . .

unaware that something *truly* awful

was about to happen.

This.

When Teddy returned home,
he immediately spotted a problem.

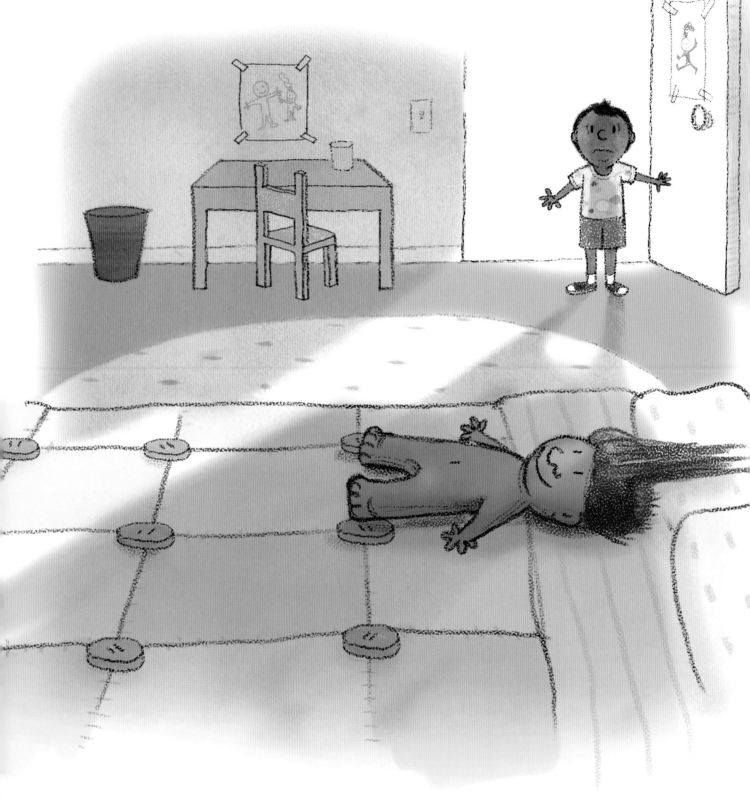

He searched for Bren-Da
in all of the likeliest places . . .

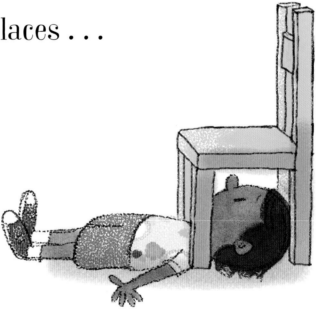

but nothing.

He sought out
his mom
and detailed
the situation.

Oh no!

OH NO!

Teddy's mom sprang into action.

Stay here!

She displayed the best manners.

Excuse me!

She performed some
impressive moves.

All the while, she looked pretty fierce.

Teddy and Bren-Da were reunited.

That night, after an extra-long bath, Teddy, Teddy's mom, and Teddy's favorite toy engaged in a most magnificent battle.

It was cool.

For Bren-Da Bowen
–C. T.

For my pal,
Alicia "Warrior Queen of Pacifica" Flannery
–M. V.

ATHENEUM BOOKS FOR YOUNG READERS • An imprint of Simon & Schuster Children's Publishing Division • 1230 Avenue of the Americas, New York, New York 10020 • Text copyright © 2018 by Christian Trimmer • Illustrations copyright © 2018 by Madeline Valentine • All rights reserved, including the right of reproduction in whole or in part in any form. • ATHENEUM BOOKS FOR YOUNG READERS is a registered trademark of Simon & Schuster, Inc. Atheneum logo is a trademark of Simon & Schuster, Inc. • For information about special discounts for bulk purchases, please contact Simon & Schuster Special Sales at 1-866-506-1949 or business@simonandschuster.com. • The Simon & Schuster Speakers Bureau can bring authors to your live event. For more information or to book an event, contact the Simon & Schuster Speakers Bureau at 1-866-248-3049 or visit our website at www.simonspeakers.com. • Book design by Lauren Rille • The text for this book was set in Garden. • The illustrations for this book were rendered in gouache and pencils and then digitally composed.
Manufactured in China
1217 SCP
First Edition
10 9 8 7 6 5 4 3 2 1
Library of Congress Cataloging-in-Publication Data
Names: Trimmer, Christian, author. | Valentine, Madeline, illustrator.
Title: Teddy's favorite toy / Christian Trimmer ; illustrated by Madeline Valentine.
Description: First edition. | New York : Atheneum, [2018] | Summary: "Teddy's favorite toy has the best manners, and the sickest fighting skills, and the ability to pull off a number of fierce looks. But when his toy goes missing, it turns out there's another woman around who's pretty fierce–it's Teddy's mom, and she will stop at nothing to reunite Teddy with his favorite toy"–Provided by publisher.
Identifiers: LCCN 2016030293
ISBN 978-1-4814-8079-6 (hardcover)
ISBN 978-1-4814-8080-2 (eBook)
Subjects: | CYAC: Toys–Fiction. | Lost and found possessions–Fiction. | Mother and child–Fiction.
Classification: LCC PZ7.1.T75 Ted 2018 | DDC [E]–dc23
LC record available at https://lccn.loc.gov/2016030293